HarperCollins®, ♣®, HarperFestival®, and Festival Readers™
are trademarks of HarperCollins Publishers Inc.
Harold and the Purple Crayon: Under the Sea
Text copyright © 2003 by Adelaide Productions, Inc.
Illustrations copyright © 2003 by Adelaide Productions, Inc.
Manufactured in China. All rights reserved.
Library of Congress catalog card number: 2002107438
www.harperchildrens.com

2 3 4 5 6 7 8 9 10
❖
First Edition

HAROLD and the PURPLE CRAYON™

Under the Sea

Text by Liza Baker
Illustrations by Kevin Murawski

HarperFestival®
A Division of HarperCollinsPublishers

It was a hot night,

and Harold couldn't sleep.

Harold wondered what he could do
to cool down.

He thought about it for some time.

Harold grew warmer and warmer.

Then he had an idea.

I know, thought Harold.

I'll go for a swim.

Harold picked up his purple crayon
and set off on an adventure.

Harold walked and walked,

searching for just the right spot.

The sun beat down on him.

The ground was cracked and dry.

Soon Harold found the perfect place.

He used his crayon to draw a puddle.

Just then, Lilac bounded up from behind.

She landed in the center of the puddle
and splashed Harold with mud.
Lilac wagged her tail playfully.

Now Harold was hot *and* dirty.

So he drew a bigger pool of water.

That way he could clean off, too.

Harold liked his new,

bigger pool but it was too calm.

So he drew some waves—

big, ocean waves.

Now he could swim.

Harold did the crawl

and Lilac did the doggy paddle.

Harold began to wonder

what was in the water.

So he drew a submarine.

Harold steered the submarine
downward,

passing fish of every

shape and size.

They saw catfish.

Lilac barked.

Then they saw dogfish.

Lilac wagged her tail.

A sawfish swam toward them.

Using its long, jagged nose,

the sawfish sawed a hole

in the side of the submarine!

Thinking quickly,

Harold drew scuba gear

for himself and Lilac.

When they reached the ocean floor,
Harold drew an underwater cave.
Just as he was about to swim inside,
he realized it wasn't a cave.

It was the open mouth of a
big-toothed fish!
Harold drew a sturdy cage around
it and swam off.

He drew a seahorse taxi.

Harold and Lilac climbed onto its back.

They sped off, leaving the scary fish

far behind.

The seahorse taxi stopped
at an old, sunken pirate ship.
Harold swam from room to room
searching for treasure.

Harold discovered an enormous chest.

It was locked, so Harold drew a key

that was just the right size.

He opened the chest.

The chest was filled with treasures!

Shiny jewels, silver coins,

and even a solid-gold dog bone.

Harold gave the bone to Lilac.

Harold realized he was tired.

Luckily, a few dolphins

were playing nearby.

They offered him a ride

to the surface.

Harold and Lilac held on tight.

The dolphins bounced Harold
and Lilac out of the water.

Back on dry land,

Harold looked up at the night sky.

The moon was shining above them.

Harold was sleepy.

He realized it was time to go home.

So he drew his bedroom window
around the moon.

Harold climbed into bed,

cool at last.

As he drifted off to sleep,

his purple crayon fell to the floor.